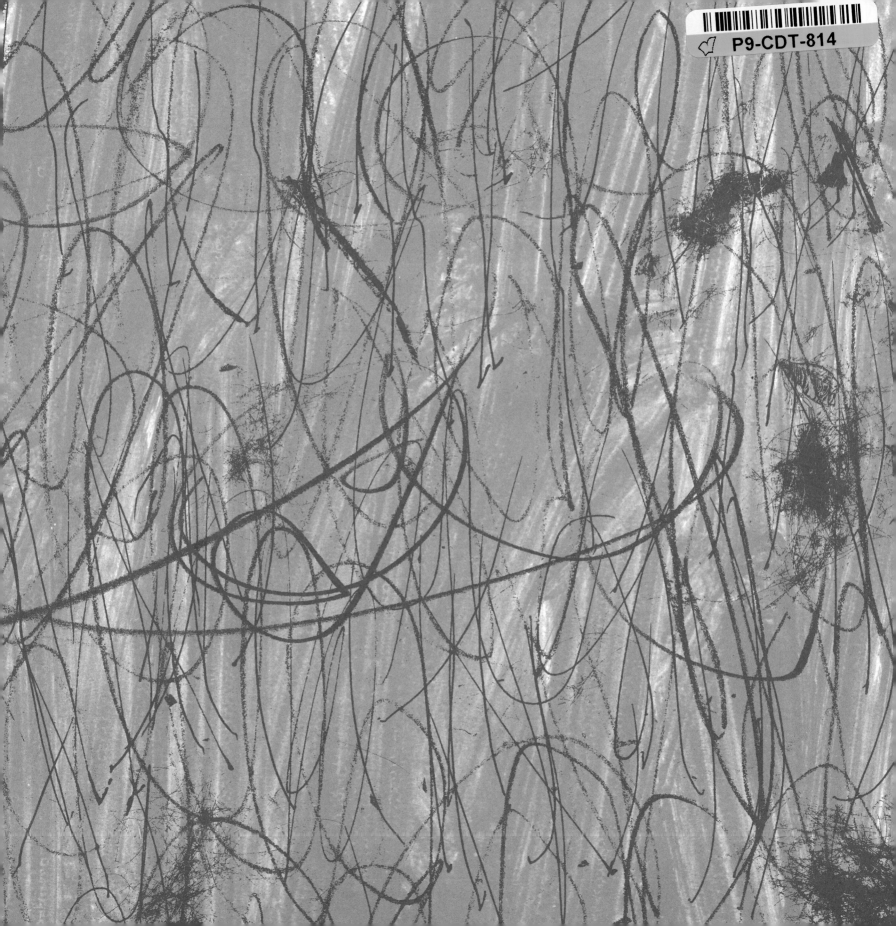

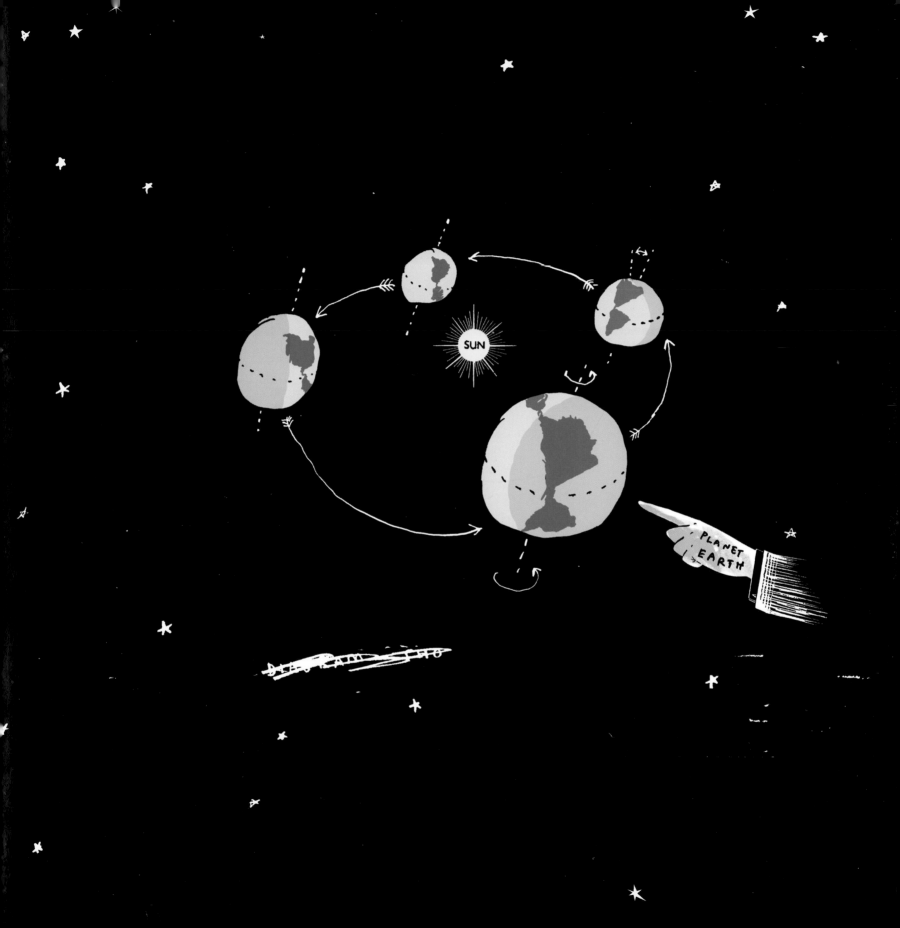

FOR SADIE AND THE KINGS HOUSE HOTEL

Copyright © 2003 by Neal Layton

First published in Great Britain by Hodder Children's Books, London

First U.S. edition 2004

Library of Congress Cataloging-in-Publication Data is available.

Library of Congress Catalog Card Number 2003051628

ISBN 0-7636-2148-X

10 9 8 7 6 5 4 3 2 1

Printed in Hong Kong

This book was typeset in Providence Sans Edu.
The illustrations were done in mixed media.

Candlewick Press
2067 Massachusetts Avenue
Cambridge, Massachusetts 02140

visit us at www.candlewick.com

HOT HOT HOT

Neal Layton

CANDLEWICK PRESS
CAMBRIDGE, MASSACHUSETTS

Meet Oscar. He's a woolly mammoth.
And so is Arabella.

They lived long ago in
a time called the Ice Age.

For most of the year it was winter.
Oscar and Arabella liked winter.

They liked the snow, the ice, and the freezing arctic winds.

But then summer would arrive.

Oscar and Arabella didn't like summer.

The sun would come out and melt all the ice and snow.

Thousands of brightly colored plants would appear from the ground, irritating their eyes and trunks.

ATCHOO!

Then there were the insects . . .

and the dust.
And this summer was worse than most.

Buzzzzz

There didn't seem to be an end in sight—it just seemed to be getting hotter
and hotter
and hotter.

Oscar found the last piece
of ice behind a rock.

But as soon as he took the ice into the sunlight, it disappeared.

And still it got **hotter**.

Arabella suggested that they find some shade under the trees.

But none of the trees was big enough.
And it got hotter still.

Oscar thought he could fan
Arabella with a big leaf.

It kept Arabella cool . . .
but made Oscar even hotter
than he had been before.

Arabella suggested that if they jumped in the lake, it might help cool them down.

PLOSH!!

But that didn't work, either.

KOF! KOF! SPLUITA!

There was only one solution.

They would have to give each other a HAIRCUT!

It was drastic, but it worked.

At last they felt cool!

When all the other animals saw them,
they decided to do the same.

The new fashion suited some animals better than others, but at least now everybody was comfortable.

Of course, summer never lasts forever. So as the world turned on its axis, winter began to set in once more.

And all the animals grew back their woolly coats.

kkk k kkkkkold!

Well, almost all the animals . . .

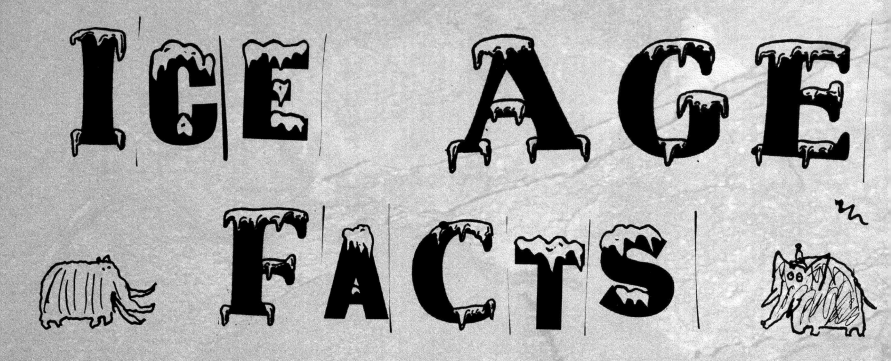

ICE AGE FACTS

There has actually been more than one ICE AGE.
Oscar and Arabella would have lived in the most recent
one, which ended about 10,000 years ago.

Seasons in the ICE AGE were much like ours, though the
summers would have been much shorter.

There probably weren't any combs, mirrors, or scissors in
the ICE AGE. I made that up. Animals would have had to
cut their woolly coats with blunt stone axes. (Just kidding.

Most scientists think there will be another ICE AGE,
but not for a few thousand years.